Music, silence,
mountains, summer.

LOVE
is everywhere!

for Charlotte Rose Ghigna & Christopher Pierce

a special thanks to Debra and Chip,
who make me believe in Love

Copyright © 2021 by Charles Ghigna & Jacqueline East

Library of Congress Control Number: 2020952546

"Schiffer Kids" logo is a trademark of Schiffer Publishing, Ltd.
Amelia logo is a trademark of Schiffer Publishing, Ltd.

Cover and interior design by Danielle D. Farmer
Type set in Fink/Avenir/Windsor

ISBN: 978-0-7643-6223-1
Printed in Serbia

Published by Schiffer Kids
An imprint of Schiffer Publishing, Ltd.
4880 Lower Valley Road
Atglen, PA 19310
Phone: (610) 593-1777; Fax: (610) 593-2002
E-mail: Info@schifferbooks.com
Web: www.schifferbooks.com

For our complete selection of fine books on this and related subjects, please visit our website at www.schifferbooks.com. You may also write for a free catalog.

Schiffer Publishing's titles are available at special discounts for bulk purchases for sales promotions or premiums. Special editions, including personalized covers, corporate imprints, and excerpts, can be created in large quantities for special needs. For more information, contact the publisher.

LOVE
is Everything

CHARLES GHIGNA

illustrated by Jacqueline East

Schiffer **Kids**™

4880 Lower Valley Road, Atglen, PA 19310

Love is everything.
I believe in love.

I believe in all the world

and all that shines above.

I believe in me.

I believe in you.

I believe in everything
that is good and true.

I believe in morning.

I believe in night.

I believe we all believe
we want to do what's right.

I believe in mountains.

I believe in trees.

I believe in sunsets
and birds that ride the breeze.

I believe in summer.

I believe in spring.

I believe in autumn,

with winter on
the wing.

I believe in music.

I believe in art.

I believe in poetry

that speaks straight from the heart.

I believe in silence.

I believe in song.

I believe that all we need
is love to get along.

I believe in daydreams
and wishes that come true.

I believe in everything.

I believe in you.